P9-DOC-138

Park Forest Public Library
400 Lakewood Blvd.
Park Forest, IL 60466

WITHDRAWN

Muddle & Mo

Nikki Slade Robinson

CLARION BOOKS
Houghton Mifflin Harcourt
Boston New York

Clarion Books
3 Park Avenue
New York, New York 10016

Copyright © 2015 by Nikki Slade Robinson

First published in New Zealand in 2015 by Duck Creek Press,
an imprint of David Ling Publishing Ltd.
First U.S. edition, 2017

All rights reserved. For information about permission to reproduce selections from this book,
write to trade.permissions@hmhco.com or to Permissions, Houghton Mifflin Harcourt Publishing Company,
3 Park Avenue, 19th Floor, New York, New York 10016.

Clarion Books is an imprint of Houghton Mifflin Harcourt Publishing Company.

www.hmhco.com

Library of Congress Cataloging-in-Publication Data is available.

ISBN 978-0-544-71612-4

Manufactured in China
SCP 10 9 8 7 6 5 4 3 2 1
4500627531

FEB 1 4 2017

BT

Dedicated to Goat, Duckie, Moon,
and their people-mummies, Maria and Sophie

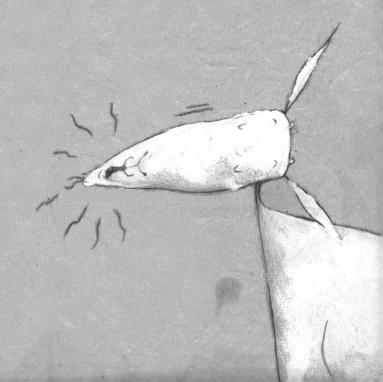

"Mo?"

"You're a funny color
for a duck!"

"Your beak is too hairy."

"You should eat worms."

"Your wings are
on your head."

"Your feet don't waddle."

"You have a wonky tail."

"And you quack funny."

"You're not a duck!
You're a goat!"

"Mo?"

"Yes, Muddle?"

"Am I a goat?"

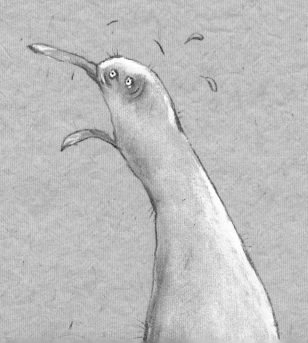

"No, Muddle.

You are one hundred percent duck.

And you will always be a duck."

"Oh. Thank you, Mo!"

The End!